The Worldly Adventures of Nicholaas

BETTY DAVIS

Reviews

Is reading the most amazing adventure of all adventures? Betty Davis thinks so. Nicholaas' worldly adventures on his sea voyage to his new home in Leiden, Holland is so vividly written, Betty takes you by the hand and you won't stop reading this book. It moved me. Why? My first name is Nicolaas and my family originated from Leiden (15th century!). I came home too.

Nico Smaling, author and publisher of stories for children: www.uitgeverijpluis.nl

So much excitement going on in Nicholaas' life! Nicholaas is a 10 year old boy who loves adventure. You will follow his fantastic voyage to Leiden, Holland by cruise ship with his Mom and Dad. He takes you on a new adventure in every port the ship docks in on the way to Holland. Join him in Funchal, Madeira, France, Belgium and Holland. Debra Walter Parent and Blogger

The Crypto-Capers Review The first in a series of fiction adventure for children 10 and up is filled with suspense and excitement. Children journey with Nicholaas as he travels to many different countries. Children enjoy the many curious and interesting facts about each country and learns about the different cultures. Renee Hand

This is a children's book review blog, and a chance for readers to keep up with their favorite books in the Crypto-Capers and Joe-Joe Nut Series. This is also a platform for the Stories From Unknown Author's Radio Show.

Copyright © 2012 Betty Davis
All rights reserved.

ISBN: 1463646992
ISBN-13: 9781463646998

I dedicate this book to my Dad
who gave me the gift and passion for writing,
and to my Mom, who gave me the
encouragement; and the idea to
write this book.

Acknowledgements

I acknowledge Jeremy Ruiz for the cover illustration.
and Annemarie Zelasko for the photo.

Contents

Chapter 1	The Great Adventure	1
Chapter 2	My Dad the Navigator	5
Chapter 3	On Board the Ship	9
Chapter 4	First Stop: Half Moon Cay, Bahamas	17
Chapter 5	Seven Days at Sea	21
Chapter 6	Funchal, Madeira	27
Chapter 7	Cherbourg, France	39
Chapter 8	Belgium	45
Chapter 9	Holland: Our New Home	55

The Great Adventure

"Oh, wow, I can't believe how ENORMOUS the ship is!" exclaimed Nicholaas. His brown hair blew furiously in the wind, tossing his cap to a nearby sandy beach. Nicholaas ran after his favorite purple and white cap, with the words Eden Prairie Football written on it. He clutched hard to his favorite notebook. He couldn't risk losing it with his all time favorite football player Adrian Peterson – a running back from Minneapolis, Minnesota on the front cover.

He had always used his notebook to remember the many different plays in football. But now his knuckles stung with pain from holding his notebook so tight. He trembled in fright, over the thought of losing either his hat or notebook.

The notebook had special significance to him, because it was his only connection with his hometown – Eden Prairie, home of the Minnesota Vikings professional football team.

The Great Adventure

Now, he and his family would be living in Holland, 4,124.38 miles away from his many friends he held dear in his heart.

Instead, he would be using the notebook as his journal, to record all the curious and interesting facts about his great adventure. For instance, he had already calculated that the ship was 719 feet long. "That's just short of two football fields. Wow!" he thought to himself.

Nicholaas' love for playing football is how he had been able to maintain his muscular build and thin frame. That did not stop the strong gusty winds from whipping across his body and nearly blowing him into anyone in front of him. Nicholaas decided to hold his notebook under his arm, to protect it better from the wind.

Now, Nicholaas stood in amazement at the sight of the ship. His large brown eyes beamed with excitement at each step he took closer. His hurried gait was temporarily stalled by the crowd of people lined up ahead of him.

It had been a long journey from his hometown of Eden Prairie, Minnesota to reach the port in Tampa, Florida partly because the airline's flight schedule had been delayed due to a patch of stormy weather. So instead of a two hour and thirty-seven minute flight, the duration was extended to nearly a four-hour flight. That can be awfully tiring for a ten year old waiting in great anticipation for the adventure to begin.

Nicholaas thought to himself, it's 1309 miles to Tampa from Minnesota, so the plane would have to fly at the speed of five hundred miles per hour!

While waiting to board Nicholaas contemplated what it would be like to travel on a ship for twelve days. He had never traveled out of the United States and he wondered what life would be like, living in Holland. During the journey, it would dock at Half Moon Cayman Islands, Funchal Madeira, Cherbourg, France, Zeebrugge, Belgium, and finally, Amsterdam, Netherlands. Nicholaas' father was an expert navigator for KLM Airlines, and he had flown a great many trips throughout Europe. But the greatest adventure awaited Nicholaas and his family, as they prepared to move to a new home in Leiden, Holland.

My Dad the Navigator

Ever since Nicholaas's dad was a young boy, he had always been interested in traveling abroad. To his father, traveling abroad was the ultimate adventure. He loved to read maps, researching interesting facts about each foreign land and imagining traveling to all of them, some day. Nicholaas remembered his dad recalling how he contemplated, with excitement, which country would be the most intriguing when he was a young boy about Nicholaas's age.

Would it be a country like Spain, France, or Holland; countries that he would, one day, visit? His dad Johan, among his friends was known as an avid reader. He spent hour upon hour discovering the many interesting facts about each country's history and culture.

After anticipating a visit to the library, sometimes two or three times per week he eagerly, searched for a new book to read. He learned all about the Eiffel Tower in France, the early history of Spain, and the great many windmills in Holland that pump the country's dykes.

He would make comments to his mom, stating things like, "If we lived in Holland, when the water freezes, people could take a day off of work or school and ice skate in the many canals in Holland. Isn't that incredible, Mom?"

Johan would even act the part by dressing up with a cap and wooden shoes that had belonged to his grandfather. On another occasion, he would dress as a chef and proclaim himself the finest chef in the world, because he is French, and France is known to have some of the greatest cooks.

As Johan grew, his interests in Geography, History, and Math blossomed. It is no wonder that he became a navigator for KLM Airlines. Now, he frequents countries that he often read and dreamed about – Spain, France, Belgium, and yes, Holland, too. His coworkers call him Captain John, because of his recent advancement to head of the navigation department. Probably, the most spectacular event in his life was the opportunity to live and work in Holland. Nicholaas's dad had many ancestors that lived in the Netherlands, as far back as the 1620's. So, Nicholaas was not the only one who was really excited about this new adventure.

Nicholaas shook with amazement, first at the size of the ship, and secondly, anticipating living in Leiden. Leiden was where the Pilgrims lived for a while, running a printing press in the early – seventeenth century, before departing to The New World.

On Board the Ship

Finally, the long anticipated wait was over. "Oh, my gosh! No way! This is so awesome! Look, it even has a writing table, and a window instead of a porthole, and a basket of goodies!"

Of course, writing was Nicholaas' favorite pastime, so his father made sure there was a room especially for him. There was even a flat screen TV and a computer for online access.

"Now I can keep in touch with my friends through emails," Nicholaas thought to himself. Nicholaas found his favorite Nocciomiele biscuits, made with nuts and honey imported from Italy. His mom, being of Italian descent, understood his love for those biscuits. There was also a wonderful supply of exotic fruits and mango juice.

On Board the Ship

He hurried into the bedroom, where he saw another basket: this one was filled with chocolates and a schedule of events especially for kids. His curiosity led him to remember a book that had been his Dad's when he was ten years old. It was set right next to some enormous, fluffy pillows. Now at the same age, Nicholaas's father had given him a book about Holland. Nicholaas knew he would treasure this book, because it has been in the family for a very long time. Now, he could learn about the history and culture of his ancestors.

The beds were really comfortable, the kind you can bounce on and feel like you're sitting on a cloud. After getting settled in the stateroom, Mom and Dad decided to take a short nap.

Of course, he was too excited to think about taking a nap, and was very curious to see what new treasures he might find in the book Dad had given him. He couldn't believe some of the fascinating things he read. For example, children living in Holland learn to swim at an early age to prevent drowning in the canals surrounding the city. Nicholaas was already a great swimmer. He had taken lessons, at Eden Prairie Park District when he was only four years old.

Nicholaas had read the events calendar, and knew there was a pool on the Promenade Deck on the ship. He thought when his mom awoke, they could explore their surroundings and take a quick swim.

On Board the Ship

It was three o'clock in the afternoon when Nicholaas and his mom decided to explore the many activities on the ship. Their first stop was the Exploration Café. The menu sold coffee, hot chocolate, delicious cakes, and cookies. The café also had a library for children and adults, as well as online access.

"Wow! Mom, look…some more books about Holland… and look, another book on the subject of the Minnesota Vikings – my favorite football team! What are the chances of finding TWO books that I'm so passionate about on this ship?"

"You are one lucky young man," answered his mom.

"After a swim, can I come back here?" asked Nicholaas. "I want to spend more time finding out interesting facts to put in my journal."

"Of course you can, but don't you want to visit the game center, so you can attend a dance for pre-teens?" asked Mom.

"Thanks, Mom, but I really am more interested in finding out more about Leiden, and what they do for fun there. I wonder if Leiden has a football team?" "Certainly!" Mom replied, as they headed in the direction of the Promenade Deck, "You can go back to the café. You just have to promise to remember to ring the 'house phone.' An assistant will bring you back to our stateroom, when you're ready. The ship does not allow children to walk around the ship alone even if you are ten years old."

"Wow, the pool is so HUGE!" Nicholaas yelled. "Come on in, the temperature is just right." In truth the water was so cold his lips were turning blue, but he continued swimming, and racing around with other children of his age in the pool. Lily, Nicholaas' Mom, was not an avid swimmer. She wrapped an orange tube around herself, after getting used to the cold water, and then floated slowly around the pool.

Lily did not have Nicholaas sense of adventure. In fact, she was having a pretty terrible experience, but did not want to show it in front of Nicholaas. When Lily was much younger, she had almost been swept away in an undertow while swimming in a lake with her family. Luckily, her dad was nearby and saved her from what could have been a tragic event.

After a short swim Lily and Nicholaas dried off, and headed back to the Exploration Café as promised, so Nicholaas could do more research. Then, Lily headed back to the stateroom in preparation for dinner.

"Remember Nicholaas, if you need an assistant to get back to your room just press star 1000 on the phone, or just call us, and we will come to get you", instructed Mom. "Sure, Mom, don't worry so much," he replied.

An hour quickly passed, after Nicholaas returned to the café. To Nicholaas, who was so intent on reading, it seemed only a short ten minutes had gone by. Now, his stomach was grumbling terribly, so he was anxious to get help, an assistant to take him back to the room, just in time for a 5:30 pm dinner.

"We have three dining rooms to pick from," began Lily, reading the itinerary. "We could eat at the Pan-Tamarind Asian Restaurant, where there is a panoramic view of the ocean: or the Pinnacle Grill, that offers cooking lessons, by an expert chef from France: or The Den, offering simple sandwiches, hamburgers and soup."

"No way, you've got to be kidding me!" said Nicholaas excitedly. "Remember only a few years ago, I dressed up in that chef hat Dad gave me? I was raving about the French being the very best cooks, in the world, just like you did Dad when you were my age. Now we're able to sample delicious food cooked by a chef from France. Sweet!"

Of course, their first evening on the ship, they enjoyed French cuisine. Every night a different ethnic food was featured, with authentic foods from Asia, Germany, Spain, France, and, of course, America.

"No way, are you kidding me?" exclaimed Nicholaas, "Look at all this food!"

"Bon Soir" announced a waiter (this means 'good evening' in French), as he passed by, and asked us to sample from the many choices on the menu.

It was hard to choose when all the food smelled and looked so delicious. Nicholaas decided on the crêpes, filled with cheese, and topped with butter and brown sugar. His parents chose pasta with a very creamy white sauce. No dinner would be complete without dessert. Nicholaas chose the strawberry shortcake, and Lily and Johan chose a sweet, delicate chocolate puff. It was so small; it was gone in one bite.

"Oh, so good!" Mom exclaimed joyfully, some chocolate still left on her lips.

"Wow, what an awesome first day! I'm amazed by the size of the ship and the stateroom, a writing table in my room, goodies, a book about Holland that I'll always treasure, and even a chef from France that will be cooking dinner the whole trip!" As he settled down for the night, Nicholaas wondered what new adventures he would discover, as he and his parents continued their journey to Holland. The next morning, the sun seemed to rise earlier than Nicholaas was used to. He awoke to the sound of the waves crashing against the ship, the same crashing waves that had helped put him to sleep the night before. It was the first thing he heard when the brilliant rays of the sun penetrated the stateroom, making it difficult to sleep any longer.

He decided to have some mango juice and his favorite Noccilmele biscuit for a quick breakfast. Nicholaas and his Dad planned to play a game of basketball in the gymnasium, while Mom spent some time on the computer looking for new and innovative ways to design clothes. Lily was a professional fashion designer, and was always looking to invent new fashions in her spare time. Most of her time was taken up with sewing elegant dresses for her clientele. Each of her dresses was one of a kind. Lily's business gave her the freedom to be home for all Nicholaas' activities and still be able to work at something she loved.

"This ship is a city!" shouted Nicholaas, "There are crowds of people everywhere, as if you were at Disneyworld, except that it's a floating resort! "We'd better get back to our stateroom, son. The itinerary states that the ship will be docking in Half Moon Cay soon," Nicholaas's Dad said in a hurried voice.

Nicholaas and Johan fought to get past the great many people who were also preparing to go ashore. They were zigging and zagging around all the passengers who also planned to exit the ship. Just imagine the number of people that attend a professional football game, and you will have a good idea about the size of the crowds of people on the Ms. Ryndam Cruise ship.

First Stop: Half Moon Cay, Bahamas

The voice of the ship's captain was loud over the speaker system "WE WILL BE STOPPING IN HALF MOON CAY. THOSE OF YOU WHO WOULD LIKE TO VISIT MAY DO SO NOW. PLEASE BE BACK PROMPTLY, AS THE SHIP SAILS AT FIVE O'CLOCK."

"Let's hurry and get our swim suits, towels, and sunglasses, so we can spend the day at the beach," Dad said in an excited tone, "I have read that the beaches are spectacular, and we won't want to miss this opportunity to swim in the ocean, and catch some sun."

Nicholaas loved to swim and could not wait to see what Half Moon Cay had to offer. He made sure to bring his notebook, so he could record all the important and curious facts about the Bahamas.

First Stop: Half Moon Cay, Bahamas

His Mom already had everything packed when they got back to the stateroom.

There were so many activities to choose from it was hard to decide, horseback riding on the beach, and even snorkeling where you could see the different species of fish. If you are feeling more adventurous there was swimming with the stingrays (not the kinds of stingray that stings or kills – these are tamed), Nicholaas said in an enthusiastic tone.

Even Mom seemed to have a sense of adventure today. Mom chose to wear a life jacket, even though the water was not deep, while using the float boards for snorkeling. They only swam out a short way, before they began to see schools of tropical fish, of nearly every color. Nicholaas' favorite was the angelfish or Pomacanthus Maculosus, the most beautiful fish you could imagine.

Angelfish have bright colors. Some blue mixed with yellow others grey and green. They actually took food from their hands. Sharks, lobsters, conches, and the stingrays were further out in the ocean. They would have to take a boat ride to see them.

"It's a good thing I remembered to bring my water resistant camera," stated Nicholaas proudly.

"Good thinking, son" said Dad with a smile.

Later, Mom went back to shore while Johan and Nicholaas put on different snorkeling gear and swam out further, to see the remains of a sunken pirate ship.

First Stop: Half Moon Cay, Bahamas

While they were unable to go all the way down to view the ruins of the ship to investigate, the Caribbean Sea was crystal clear. So clear, they could see the ruins through their masks submerged a little under the surface.

"The water is so clear, I can see my reflection," remarked Nicholaas, as they headed back to shore. While other members of the ship were still swimming with the stingrays or riding horses on the beach, his parents helped Nicholaas build a small Viking ship in the sand. They did their best to make a miniature replica, similar to the one on display at the Minnesota Vikings training facility.

The Minnesota Vikings' antique ship has been restored and sits out in front of their training center, as a symbol of their spirit and mental toughness.

As the day at Half Moon Cay was coming to an end, Nicholaas walked off quickly to change into dry clothes, and brushed all the sand off himself as he did so. With each step, his diving shoes made a squish-squashing sound. He wanted to spend some time in the lounge chair, writing about the exciting events of the day before heading back to board the ship.

Nicholaas settled in a lounge chair that seemed rather uncomfortable, at first. It was the kind of chair that had plastic straps over the full length of the chair, but a few of them were worn and loose. By the condition of the chair, it was evident that it had been out in the elements for quite a while.

Nicholaas wrote about the exciting events of the day: the Viking ship he and his parents made, the angelfish he fed and photographed, and the ruins of a pirate ship seen through crystal clear water. Now, his anticipation grew with the thought of their next stop in Funchal, Madeira Island.

Seven Days at Sea

The next morning, Nicholaas awoke to the sound of seagulls screeching, "Psssooo, Pssoooo, Awk, Awk". A distant, low sound that would become piercingly high, then low again, as they swooped down and then flew up. The gulls were flying low, looking for their next meal. Seagulls eat just about anything. He read that seagulls will even eat fries right out of your hand. Today, they were happy with fish.

Now, for the next seven days, Nicholaas was preoccupied with his favorite activities of swimming and writing. Whenever he left the stateroom, he always wore his favorite purple and white Eden Prairie football cap, along with his backpack. The bag contained his notebook, camera, pen, and towel for swimming. Nicholaas always wanted to be ready to capture any new or curious treasures.

Each morning after a quick swim, Nicholaas would spend a few hours at the Exploration Café. He loved the smell of cocoa and warm pastries, right out of the oven.

"I would like a warm apple slice and some hot cocoa with whipped cream, please," he politely instructed.

His eyes danced with excitement at each bite. As Nicholaas finished his hot cocoa and wiped off his mouth with a nearby napkin, he noticed a rather tall boy with the same muscular frame sitting near the computers, wearing a shirt that had 'Leiden Holland' printed on it.

"Whoa, no way," Nicholaas thought to himself, "That's where my family will be living." He couldn't contain himself any longer, and in his excitement he blurted out, "Hello, I'm Nicholaas, and I'm going to be living in Leiden, Holland!"

The words raced out of his mouth, as if he were in a contest to see who could talk the fastest. The boy was rather shy, and with a deep voice said "Greetings, I'm Chris!" His eyes also shined with excitement. "I have lived in Leiden for as long as I can remember," announced Chris. "I have never been to the United States, so my family decided to take a trip to Disneyworld in Orlando, Florida, before we move the city of Funchal".

Nicholaas was amazed at the coincidence. "No way! This is my first trip on a ship, and we are relocating to Leiden, Holland because my dad accepted a position as Head of the Navigation Department of KLM Airlines in Amsterdam."

"There is so much history to explore in Leiden. I am sure you will absolutely love it!" Chris said, with enthusiasm.

"I am originally from Eden Prairie, Minnesota", said Nicholaas.

"I believe that Kristi Yagamucci lives in Eden Prairie. She won the gold medal in 1992 for figure skating," responded Chris. "Ice skating is very popular in Holland," he continued, "and when the canals around Holland freeze, everyone comes out of their homes to ice skate."

"I think that Leiden is similar to Eden Prairie, with its rolling hillsides and plentiful lakes," said Chris. "Leiden is a very old city dating back to 1572 when Leiden sided with the Dutch in fighting Spanish rule. The Dutch were liberated in 1648. Although, some of the earliest settlers from England, called Pilgrims, first came to Leiden and operated a printing press before they moved on to Massachusetts."

"Wow, oh my gosh, how awesome! I love to investigate and discover new things," said Nicholaas.

Suddenly, his mind was elsewhere. "Hey, do they have a football team in Leiden? I played football when I lived in Eden Prairie, and it's one of my favorite sports. Our team was chosen to visit the Minnesota Vikings training facility and play a game with the pros!" said Nicholaas, his pride showing on his face. "The Vikings choose one team each year, one they feel is the best team and shows good sportsmanship. It was the most amazing experience in my whole life, to be able to play on the same field that the pros practice on". "Football is the most popular sport in Holland. More people love football than any other sport, with soccer and ice skating coming in second and third. They have a football club that travels to Amsterdam, "Chris continued, "Football is played differently in Holland than in America. For instance, they use fewer players in the younger leagues, and the number of players increases as they progress through the league."

"I never played football myself, but my best friend Pieter does. He is a receiver for the Cubs and plays on the twelve-year-olds' team. The thirteen- to fifteen year- olds play on the team called the Cadets. Chris explained. Chris looked wistful for a minute, "I miss Pieter badly. He intends to visit Funchal in a few months, after we get settled. It's funny you mentioned about the training facility. My Mom talked about visiting that very place, long ago. She has a distant cousin that lives in Eden Prairie and they visited the training facility there together."

"Oh my gosh, no way! Are you kidding'? What's their name? Where do they live now?" Nicholaas asked excitedly.

"It is a long time ago, but I think his name is something like…Jake, no…Jeremy…no John, no…Johan, that's it!" exclaimed Chris.

"No way! My Dad's name is Johan! Can it be true, we might be related? Let's go find our parents and find out for sure! This could be great news!" Nicholaas suggested. After sharing the thrilling news with their parents, who became as excited as the boys were, the two decided to go back to the café, where they could talk and listen to music on the computers. It seemed they talked non-stop for more than three hours. It was nearly five o'clock, and they both needed to go back and prepare for dinner.

The next day, the ship would dock in Funchal, Madeira Island. Time was flying by so quickly. It seemed that Nicholaas had just met his distant cousin, Chris, and he and his family would be disembarking the ship to live in Madeira. Nicholaas wished he could stop time, so he could get to know his new found relative better. They had so much in common, and he was so excited to have met him.

As Nicholaas reflected on yet another adventure, he was so glad his parents decided to move to Holland, allowing him to meet his distant cousin, Chris.

Chris promised his family would be visiting Leiden often, to visit Nicholaas and his friend, Pieter. Nicholaas' parents were very excited about the prospect of the boys reuniting, and spending days with them. They would plan regular trips to Madeira Island.

Funchal, Madeira

Nicholaas awoke every day to the sounds of seagulls flying by, or the waves hitting the boat, but this morning he got up early to get prepared for the adventures that the day would bring. The ship would dock in Funchal, Madeira for only eight hours.

Nicholaas' daily visits to the café were where each new adventure began. Today, he ran to get a slice of apple pie and a glass of lemonade. He looked for exciting and interesting facts about the Island of Madeira. For instance, Nicholaas read in a magazine called Portugal. BZ that it is 56 kilometers long and 19 kilometers wide, but it would take a day to drive around the entire island due to volcanic peaks that rise up 1,862 meters. "Wow," thought Nicholaas to himself, "the Island must have a lot of winding and narrow roads." He read on. "Madeira Island is in the

Atlantic ocean, about 600 kilometers from Morocco, and about 1000 miles from Lisbon, Portugal. Probably the most fascinating fact is that records indicate a ship, carrying the famous pirate William Kidd (called Captain Kidd) and his immense treasure sank in a location close to Deserted Island, which is not far from Madeira."

"How lucky Chris is, to live on an island with so much adventure," he thought.

Nicholaas read more. "Pirates invaded Porto Santo and Deserted Island back in 1476. Christopher Columbus married Felipa Palestro Moniz, a member of a wealthy Portuguese family. Christopher Columbus later moved with his wife and child, Diego, to the larger island of Madeira."

Nicholaas' mind raced, as he tried to plan activities and, somehow, make time stand still. Nicholaas was excited to explore with his cousin today, but also sad they would be going their separate ways. The moment the two boys met there had been an instant connection.

"According to the ship's captain, the temperature will be in the low eighties, with a few clouds. April is normally the rainy season, so we are fortunate to have good weather," Nicholaas thought.

He checked his backpack, making sure he had his towel, swimsuit, camera, notebook, and pen. This time he added a flashlight. "Never know when this might come in handy to read in the dark," he said proudly. As he was confident that he was prepared for anything. He also made sure to include the trading card of his all time favorite NFL football player Adrian Peterson, autographed by the star himself. Nicholaas planned to give the card to Chris, as a memento of the time they had spent together on this trip.

Nicholaas' parents were finalizing what they needed for the day, and then they would meet up with Chris and his parents.

"Wow. Mom, Dad, look! The mountains have so much green and there are so many wild flowers, you can't even see rock!" exclaimed Nicholaas.

"Cool!" Chris replied, "The clouds look like they are touching the peaks of the mountains."

The captain of the Ms. Ryndam explained, "The weather here is so moderate because the island is surrounded by mountains. People swim and enjoy nature the whole year through, although April is the rainy season."

"Volcano eruptions, a very long time ago, shaped this island into what it is today," the captain continued. Nicholaas was very anxious to start exploring; his head was spinning with excitement. After reviewing the itinerary, both Nicholaas and Chris' parents agreed that they wanted to explore by foot. As they traveled through the long, narrow, and often winding, pathways, they were greeted by the smell of flowers, abundantly lining the cobblestone streets. There were flowers of every color, including some exotic ones such as Bird of Paradise and Orchids.

Each apartment and storefront, in the historical part of Funchal, gave you the feeling that an artisan had taken a very long time to build them, carving each stone with exquisite detail. The stone and brick seemed several hundred years old at least. Of course, none of the older apartments have the modern conveniences that most of us are used to, like air conditioning or updated electrics.

The group continued on their journey, listening to the sounds of the waves and the smell of flowers that appeared everywhere they went. Then, suddenly, right before them, they saw a huge balloon – a hot air balloon.

"This is the most perfect day ever to go up!" Chris and Nicholaas shouted in unison.

After purchasing their tickets, all of them boarded the balloon. No one there had ever ridden in a hot air balloon before, so they were all anxiously awaiting the release of the ropes from the dock. Soon the air ship was ready to launch. The sky was becoming much cloudier then, when they first docked in Funchal.

Again, Nicholaas' thoughts were spinning with excitement! He couldn't wait to see what adventure they would encounter next, as the balloon rose higher and higher into the sky. The balloon soared to its maximum height: one hundred and fifty feet. Everyone seemed to be enjoying the magnificent view, but then there was a horrible sound. "UUGH!!"

The sound came from a nearby passenger who had become violently ill. All of a sudden, there was a "thump,

thump, thump," as the wind violently whipped and tore at the balloon. Nicholaas turned around and noticed the sky had turned from partly cloudy to the blackness of an impending storm, in a matter of minutes.

All thirty people that had boarded the balloon were now being thrown around the gondola like toys. Sounds of terrifying screams were everywhere around the airship, while others prayed that everyone would get down safely.

"Hold on tight son, we will be okay!" Dad shouted.

The strong gusts of wind continued to cause damage to the envelope, creating increasingly larger tears in the nylon panels. The captain stopped the burner, so the balloon would lose buoyancy and descend as quickly as possible. Nicholaas's Mom was terrified and shaking with fear that the balloon, and everyone in it, would crash into the ocean below. Mom tried desperately not to panic, even though she had a fear of water and would not be able to swim.

Lightning lit up the skies. Thunder rumbled all around them. "Only fifty feet to go!" shouted the captain. "Everyone, get down on the floor to help balance the basket."

As the wind barreled into them, Nicholaas also worried that they would be pushed out of the wicker basket. Torrential rain pierced the sky, and each raindrop felt like a pellet pounding on their bodies.

It was three-thirty in the afternoon, but it seemed later. The sky was dark with bolts of lightning zigzagging in the sky. The balloon skidded and bounced with a hard thump. It took five men to restrain it. By grasping the tie lines, and anchoring the craft, tying ropes to sturdy posts, it allowed the group to leave safely. As the passengers disembarked the air ship, each step toward escape seemed to take every ounce of strength they had.

There was no way they could attempt to return to the Ms. Ryndam, with wind gusts of up to fifty miles per hour. They knew they had to find shelter right away!

"Where can we go? What should we do?" shouted Nicholaas to his dad.

"Look ahead," announced Chris, "it looks like an old mansion. Let's see if anyone can help us."

The mansion was set back on a hilltop, one hundred yards away. The terrifying elements of the storm made it difficult to walk; it seemed like it took forever to get there.

Once they reached the door of the mansion Nicholaas's Dad yelled "Everyone push!" The immense wooden door was well worn, as though it had not been used in many years. There was no doorbell, just two old metal knobs on each of the two doors. The kind of door you might see in an old movie.

"Push harder!" someone yelled. Finally they were able to open the door enough to enter the house, and get out of the cold wind and rain. "We need to find a way of getting some light in here, so we can get warm and find our way back to the ship," Johan said, taking the lead. "I see a glimpse of light coming from somewhere over there: it looks like a doorway or something," Nicholaas volunteered. As they edged their way to the doorway, the floor creaked, "eek eek", with each step they took.

Nicholaas suddenly remembered adding a flashlight to his list of items kept in his backpack. "I wonder why I included this today, of all days?" thought Nicholaas to himself, as he pulled the flashlight out and clicked it on.

Nicholaas directed the beam from the flashlight slowly around the room. He and Chris saw the most amazing room, filled with sports memorabilia. The first thing the light shown upon was an old helmet. Nicholaas and Chris scampered across the room, to take a closer look. It was an old football helmet. The kind worn way back in the early days of football, maybe even the first one! It was a black leather cap held on with straps under the chin. Not at all like the sophisticated helmets they have today. Nicholaas hurried to try it on.

"Oh my gosh!" Chris blurted, as he spied something else on the shelf, "Look at this, a football." Chris snatched it from the shelf. "What? Holey moley – it's signed by Walter Payton of the Chicago Bears!"

As Chris threw the ball to Nicholaas, they were both immediately whisked down a dark secret tunnel and landed on what seemed like an exact replica of the Minnesota Vikings stadium – the Hubert Humphrey Metro dome.

"What happened, where are we?" Nicholaas wondered, a little dazed.

They both looked at each other in amazement. As they started walking onto the field they stumbled across the football Walter Payton had signed, and again they held onto it. The stadium was enormous, the size and the seating capacity just like the stadium back home. The grass was artificial turf, like the pros use.

"Let's play a game of touch football!" suggested Nicholaas.

"How can we play with only two of us?" Chris asked.

"Let's play, there's something magical about this place," urged Nicholaas.

Chris kicked the football to the thirty-yard line. Nicholaas retrieved the ball. As he was racing toward the goal line, he saw Walter Payton, known as "sweetness" to his fans, running right beside him.

"Weave to your left, now right... stay low," instructed Payton. Nicholaas could not believe his eyes. "I must be dreaming. How can this be true?" Nicholaas thought to himself.

Nicholaas was panting furiously by the time he reached the goal line for a touchdown.

"What's the matter, Nicholaas, why are you so out of breath? You only ran twenty yards," Chris asked.

"What? No way! Didn't you see him?"

"Who?" asked Chris.

"Walter Payton!" gasped Nicholaas, still out of breath.

"There's no one out here but you and me. Throw the ball, and let's play," suggested Chris, ignoring what Nicholaas had said.

Nicholaas threw the ball and prepared to play defense, when all of sudden, Brian Piccolo stood beside him. "Stay committed to what your passion is, and you will be successful."

Nicholaas looked again and no one was there. He looked to the edge of the field and, in the stands, saw a crowd of people cheering. Nicholaas wondered if he was just imagining things, or had he really seen Walter Payton, Brian Piccolo, and the fans cheering?

"Chris... Nicholaas... Where are you?" He and Chris heard their parents calling.

"Over here!" Chris and Nicholaas chimed. They turned around, and the stadium was gone. They were in the cellar of the abandoned house. "Open the door!" they heard from the other side of a hatch. The boys rushed to push the door open, and light streamed in as the portal gave way. The storm had died down. "Hurry, we've got to get back to the ship. We're two hours late. I called ahead, and they are waiting for us."

"Okay, give me a minute," Nicholaas replied as he tore through his backpack, which was damp, but not soaked.

"I want you to have this. It's an autographed card of Adrian Peterson, as a memento of our friendship," Nicholaas said, offering his gift.

Chris' eyes watered up, "Let's not say goodbye. We will be visiting Holland once we have settled in to our own houses. I will contact Pieter, and let him know to look for you, once you reach Leiden."

With a handshake and a compadre hug, the two boys parted and went their separate ways.

After a very exciting, but tumultuous day, they were now headed back to the ship. Nicholaas couldn't wait to get back to his table in the room and write about the day's events.

Cherbourg-Octeville, France

Nicholaas woke to the delicious smells of cinnamon and chocolate. His mom and dad decided to have breakfast in their stateroom today, after the stormy weather that had engulfed them yesterday.

Lily wanted to surprise Nicholaas with his favorite crêpes, filled with cheese and sprinkled with cinnamon, butter, and chocolate. "Yummy!" Nicholaas shouted with excitement, "It looks and smells delicious. Thanks, Mom!"

After breakfast, Nicholaas and his dad followed their daily routine of taking a quick swim, then off to the gym to play basketball. Lily wanted to work on more new dress designs.

Lily was very innovative in her designs. She would have much more time to work, once they were settled in Leiden, Holland. For now, she was happy to just create drawings on the computer, with some notes on designs she plans to make. Lily hoped, one day, to have her own line of clothes. These days, she is happy sewing one-of-a-kind clothes or her clients. Most of her clients are quite discerning about the type of dress they would like, but she also caters to customers who need a dress on a budget or to the occasional customer, who just needs some tailoring done.

The captain announced over the speaker, "WE WILL BE DOCKING IN CHERBOURG, FRANCE, SHORTLY. WE WILL ONLY BE STAYING FOR FOUR HOURS, INSTEAD OF EIGHT. THE SEVERE STORM YESTERDAY CAUSED A DELAY IN OUR DEPARTURE FROM MADERIA. UNFORTUNATELY, THIS MEANS THAT WE MUST ABBREVIATE OUR TIME IN FRANCE. I HOPE EVERYONE WILL ENJOY THEIR SHORTENED VISIT TO CHERBOURG."

Nicholaas overheard a few passengers grumbling and groaning at the message.

One mumbled, "There's not much to do in four hours." Another exclaimed, "I'm supposed to meet a dear friend I haven't seen in years, and now my meeting will be cut short!" Almost everyone was disappointed, but they understood. It is not only promptness the captain has to consider, but also the tide that provides ample depth for a passenger ship to enter a port. So, the captain was right to think about the time tide is due in at the next port. Nicholaas and his dad hurried back to the room, to pick up

Cherbourg-Octeville, France

Nicholaas' backpack and a jacket for each of them. It was a bit chillier in France than on Madeira.

As the passengers exited the ship to head into Cherbourg-Octeville, Nicholaas noticed the weather was cloudy and that there was a fine mist of rain.

Cherbourg-Octeville lays Northwest of Paris in the Normandy Region. It is surrounded by the English Channel and is known mainly as a naval port utilized during World War II. Its most impressive site is Cite' de la Mer (City of the Sea), the city's maritime museum. It was in Cherbourg that the world's largest submarine was built, called the Redoutable S611. Nicholaas never had seen or been on a submarine before, so he was anxious to see what new adventure he would discover onboard.

"Oh, my gosh. No way!" shouted Nicholaas. "Look how narrow these hallways are!"

The Redoutable S611 had one hundred and twenty sailors, and fifteen officers. The submarine carried M2 missiles, and later M20s. Each could deliver a one-megaton warhead at a range of over three thousand kilometers. Nicholaas was fascinated at the size and history of the ship. He tried to grasp how hard it would have been for the sailors to endure the tight living quarters during their tour of duty. The sub had totaled twenty years of active duty.

After their quick visit to the museum, they located a spot that rented scooters.

"Now, we'll tour the French countryside," announced Nicholaas' Dad.

Scooters are a popular mode of transportation in France. They are small and compact, so it's easier to get around the narrow streets typical in France and other European countries. Nicholaas hopped on, after making sure his helmet was secured. Mom followed closely behind, as they started their descent into the beautiful countryside.

France has the most amazing countryside, filled with flowers and gently rolling hills. They drove past the Botanical Gardens and stopped for a quick lunch that had crepes with chocolate and cream cheese.

There was a grove of a great many apple trees as they drove past a small café, and the sweet smell of apples made Nicholaas hunger for a slice of apple pie. Nicholaas would have to wait as it was already 11:30 am, and they had to head back to the ship. As they traveled back to the city, they saw and smelled flowers of every kind and color.

"Bon Jour, bon jour!" the storekeepers would say as we drove quickly by.

The strong wind blew against Nicholaas' body, making him wrap his arms around his Dad's waist. He held so tight, he thought it might keep his Dad from breathing. "Don't hold so tight!" Mom warned. The wind was so strong and furious that Nicholaas thought he would be blown off the scooter for sure, with the slightest bump in the road. Even though the wind made him feel uncomfortable, he loved every minute of it. It was exhilarating, a ride that he would remember for a very long time.

Their visit to France was coming to an end. As the ship left the port, Nicholaas observed that the people of Cherbourg were very friendly and often used hand gestures to express themselves. His anticipation grew each day, as their final destination steadily got closer. Tomorrow the ship would dock in Belgium, the last stop before Holland. He scurried back to his room on the ship, to write down all the adventures of this eventful day.

Belgium

Nicholaas could hardly sleep at that time, with the excitement of there being only two more days until the Ms. Ryndam docked in Amsterdam. The town of Leiden is just a short ride by train from Amsterdam. So compared to the twelve- day trip on the ship, it would seem like a matter of minutes to get to his new home.

He would get excited whenever he pictured the new house they would be living in and meeting Pieter for the first time. Recently he had received an email from Chris confirming that he and his family were still planning on traveling to Lisbon, the capital of Portugal, in the summer, before heading to Holland. While in Holland, they planned to stay a few days with Nicholaas' family and a few days with Pieter.

Nicholaas longed for the day he would see Chris again. The time they had spent together had been an amazing experience; the kind you don't easily forget. He contemplated his meeting with Pieter. Chris told him so much about Pieter Nicholaas felt like he already knew him. He was two years older than Nicholaas, and enjoyed playing football. Pieter even shared the same birthday with him – December 6th.

Pieter had even made a pair of wooden shoes and carved exceptionally fine objects from wood. Chris informed him that once Pieter had made a checker set out of wood, complete with a wooden playing board.

Before the ship docked in Zeebrugge, Belgium Nicholaas wanted to make a stop at his favorite place on the ship, the Exploration Café. There he could speculate on the next adventure that he could expect to find in Belgium. Nicholaas surfed the internet and found out many interesting facts about events and the history of Belgium. He ran across some information about a medieval castle: Gravensteen.

He wondered what life might have been like in the twelfth century. He reflected: on how it would have been for the counts and knights that once live and worked in a dark, damp, cold castle? There would be neither windows, to keep out the cold air, nor electricity for light at night. A castle is a big fortress with a body of water that surrounds it, called a moat. This was the means used to keep invaders and enemies out. The dungeon was to punish those who chose to fight against the reign of the ruling lord. "N-I-C-H-O-L-A-A-S"

"Oh-oh, my parents are calling," he realized. When Nicholaas heard his parents, he hurried to get his notebook into his backpack and raced to meet them, almost tripping over a nearby chair. Many of the passengers had already gone ashore, by the time Nicholaas and his family got to the exit.

'I'm sorry, Mom, for being late. I got involved in reading about a castle called Gravensteen. Gravensteen means castle of counts. It was first built in 911 in a town called Ghent. It has a moat, a dungeon and a lookout tower!"

Luckily, he had kept his backpack with him when he went to the café. All his important items were in his backpack: his Minnesota Vikings football cards, his notebook, pen, camera, and the newest addition, a flashlight. He didn't think he would be using his swimsuit and towel again, until they were in their new home in Leiden. This was the last port the Ms. Ryndam would visit, before docking in Holland.

After a short delay, they were headed by scooter out of Zeebrugge and toward Ghent. It is nearly thirty miles, so walking is not an option. Ghent is best known for its beautiful Gothic buildings. Probably the most amazing site is the castle, and the Belfry Tower.

As they traveled through Zeebrugge, it was as if they traveled through time. Ancient buildings, surviving since the twelfth century, were everywhere.

"Wow! No way!" shouted Nicholaas. "Look how tall that tower is, and the castle is gigantic! Imagine what it would be like to live during the Middle Ages" Nicholaas stared in disbelief as he bent way back to view the ninety-one meter high tower from the scooter. The canals all around the city, and which surrounded it, added to his awe.

"Let's climb to the top!" Nicholaas blurted out excitedly, before his dad had a chance to park the scooter. "That way, we can get the best view of the city."

As Nicholaas and his family started their ascent, they found two solid stone doors, and each one had three locks. "I remember reading about where the money was stored in 1338. This is where the bells rang for the English King Edward. The story states that the door could not be opened unless one of the guilds was there and only then could the doors be opened," Nicholaas recalled, accurately.

As they continued their tour, they saw the carillon bells that would warn the town of an impending attack, or some announcement of an important event. There were always four guards assigned to lookout, and each guard would blow his horn every hour, to indicate to the whole town that everything was okay.

As they reached the top of the tower, there was a panoramic view of the entire city. You could see the beautiful Gothic buildings and the land crisscrossed everywhere with canals. It was easy to imagine what life must have been like during the medieval era. Gravensteen Castle had been built right on the water, to have easy access to food, and making it harder for invaders to attack them. Gravensteen Castle is one of the only places in Belgium where you can see the living conditions of the people during the Middle Ages. In general, castles in medieval times were used as refuges, and for harboring locals during attacks from enemies.

There were three different castles built on this very spot. One had been built out of wood in the ninth century and had protected the area from Vikings. Then, in the eleventh century, a house had been built out of stone, with the dimensions of thirty-three feet by nineteen feet, and with walls two meters thick. The third castle was erected by Count Philip of Alsace in the year 1180. Many castles similar to Gravensteen were built in other regions, to maintain control and influence over the people. Contrary to common belief, knights and counts rarely stayed overnight in the castle. In times of peace, the castle served mainly as a symbol of power and strength. The old walls surrounding him on every side provoked a sinister feeling as Nicholaas and his family walked through the gate. As they continued walking through the castle, they couldn't help feeling it was dark, damp and uninviting. The first room they saw was a big hall. It appeared to be a dining hall where all the knights and counts would gather for a feast, or plan strategies in the face of an attack.

The signs directed us to the torture room where guillotines were used as early as the twelfth century, and continued with a more improved blade into 1789.

"Look, there's an armory museum can we go there next?" Nicholaas pleaded.

"Sure, son," Mom and Dad answered in unison.

"This is sick! Look at the selection of spears, lances, swords, axes…and even crossbows! They're all displayed in individual cases!" To Nicholaas, the room no longer seemed dark and damp. Instead, it felt bright and alive. Placed next to the weapons, there was an entire suit of armor. It was the focal point of the room.

Nicholaas ran to investigate, and wondered how hard it would be to fight off enemies while wearing a metal suit.

As Nicholaas read aloud a sign about Count Philip of Alsace, he found himself in the middle of a skirmish. Townspeople had had enough of the tyranny from knights and counts and were attacking the castle. There stood Count Philip with his suit of armor, yelling, "Hey, you there," pointing Nicholaas' way, "go and get me more spears, and hurry up about it!"

"O--O--Okay" answered a startled Nicholaas.

He was scared and surprised to be in the midst of a battle. There were townspeople shooting spears and lances at the knights, piercing their bodies and throwing their

bodies into the moat below, while the knights attacked using axes, lances, and spears while trampling the peasants with their horses. Nicholaas almost got hit by one: it narrowly missed him. He felt the breeze of it, as it whizzed by! The spear landed in the leg of another count.

"Hurry up with those spears there boy. What is taking so long?"

Nicholaas hastily gathered the spears that were lying on the ground next to the injured people. He hurried to hand over the spears, when all of a sudden, he turned, and he was back at the museum.

"Mom…Dad, did you see what just happened to me?"

"Son, what do you mean, I saw you the whole time. You were standing reading the sign about the suit of armor. Maybe, you're getting hungry; let's finish up and get a bite to eat."

Nicholaas wondered whether he had just been dreaming, but when he reached in his coat pocket, something sharp slit his finger. It was a piece of spear that, somehow, had got into his pocket. He raced to the display case: he looked at where there had been two spears but now there was just one. The spearhead in his coat pocket matched the one in the case. "Ka-ching"! Nicholaas thought to himself. He would treasure this artifact forever. Mom gave him a bandage for his cut, assuming he got the cut from the rough edges of the sign.

As they exited the castle, it was once again a bright sunny day, just as it had been when they entered. Nicholaas had truly gone back in time, but it would be his secret.

Ahead, there was a café that offered Belgium fries with all types of sauces, as well as hamburgers.

"Yum, it smells great!" Nicholaas said, swooning.

Nicholaas and his family all decided to have fries and a piece of chocolate.

"This is the most awesome chocolate I ever tasted! Mom, this is my new favorite."

"Okay, let's take some Belgium chocolate back with us. It really is deep, dark and rich tasting," Mom agreed.

All the architecture in Ghent is in the Gothic style. The houses and buildings were the most beautiful of all the countries Nicholaas had visited.

Belgium is a small country, about the size of Rhode Island in the United States. It is densely populated, and has more people visiting than actually living there. The citizens of Belgium speak English very well. Tourists come from nearby countries, visiting towns like Ghent and Brussels.

His parents agreed that they could visit again. Belgium will be their neighbor and so will England. It is a strange, delightful experience to discover the history and customs of different countries.

Nicholaas couldn't wait to get back to the ship to record his adventures of the Belfry Tower and the castle, and his experience meeting the count.

Tomorrow afternoon, the ship will dock in Amsterdam. Time had seemed to fly since boarding the ship eleven days ago, and having adventures every day. But Nicholaas was also anxiously awaiting the adventures ahead – in Holland.

Holland: Our New Home

Nicholaas couldn't contain his excitement. He was just as excited as when he first boarded the Ms. Ryndam in Tampa, Florida. Now, he would be able to experience the amazing and curious things he had only read about in his most treasured book, The Worldly Adventures in Holland. It was a book he had received from his Dad the first day they were on the ship. The same book had been given to Dad, when he was the same age as Nicholaas was now.

"WE WILL BE DOCKING IN AMSTERDAM IN AN HOUR AND TWENTY MINUTES," the captain informed them.

Amsterdam is a beautiful city with elegant houses and winding canals.

While his parents were preparing for departure, Nicholaas went to the Exploration Café for his last slice of apple pie onboard the ship. He sent a quick email to Chris and Pieter, letting them know his new address in Leiden.

Their new house would have five bedrooms, plenty of room for guests when they visited. The house would be only five minutes from the Centre of Leiden. There are a great many hiking trails, museums, and flower gardens not far from their new home. Of course, for Nicholaas, no city would be complete without a sports complex for playing football.

"Oh my gosh, no way! Mom...Dad, we're here!" shouted Nicholaas with an exuberant voice. He could see the magnificent city from on board the ship. The ship edged closer to the port, as passengers bustled about getting their belongings together, preparing to depart. Amsterdam is so amazingly beautiful!" observed Nicholaas. He remembered reading about the buildings all being built right next to each other to save space. A lot of the architecture is from the 1900's, and the artistic style comes from the influence of King Louis, like the homes in Belgium. As they exited the ship, Nicholaas gave the vessel one last look and was still awed by its majestic presence; its size and beauty.

"Hurry, Nicholaas, we've got to catch the train," said Mom in a hurried tone. The train station is only a few hundred steps from where the ships docked. It would only take thirty minutes to get to Leiden. They each carried a suitcase with them when they exited the ship. The rest of the luggage and the things they will need for the next few years had already been shipped, six weeks ago. Dad mentioned that their furnishings should already be at their new home.

As they boarded the intercity train his anticipation grew, and questions raced through his mind. He reflected on what it would be like to live in Leiden, where he would go to school, and most importantly, when he would see Chris again. Nicholaas longed to see Chris, and he knew he would enjoy the company once they reunited. Chris said they would be coming out this summer, but that was at least eight weeks away. As Nicholaas' thoughts still raced around in his mind, his father's voice called. "Nicholaas, let's get off the train, now."

It had been twelve days, since Nicholaas and his family had left Eden Prairie, Minnesota, and now his new adventure would begin.

"Uh, okay Dad."

"Son, why are you so quiet, are you alright?"

"I'm fine, I was just thinking of Chris and what our house will be like."

"Oh my gosh, no way! Wow!" Nicholaas' attention was quickly diverted to a truly amazing place. "Look it's the Rembrandt Museum. Rembrandt was a famous painter and lived in Leiden for several years. Cool, another museum! Look at this book; it says here that the pilgrims came here to live in the 1700's, to run a printing press. See, this document here shows all the names of the people who were on the Mayflower, traveling to Plymouth Rock. "Of all cities in Holland, Leiden is the most interesting, and has the most history," stated Nicholaas. They had only been there one hour, and already there was so much history to explore and discover.

They started walking down the cobblestone streets, taking in all the new and wonderful sights before them. The smells of fresh flowers were everywhere.

Tulips of every color were on display, but the bright purple and white ones were his favorite. Tulips had first been developed right here at Leiden University, the oldest university in the Netherlands. The university library had three and a half million books and fifty thousand other periodicals, including maps and atlases.

The canals and bridges wind throughout the city, which only adds to the natural beauty of Leiden. Nicholaas started to drag his large, heavy suitcase behind him when he heard his father exclaim excitedly, "That looks like our new home, Nicholaas!" Nicholaas ran as fast as he could to get a closer look, leaving his suitcase behind. The house was made out of stone, and from the outside looked like a small quaint cottage. It sat right on the corner, so it was set apart from the other houses.

As they entered the house, Nicholaas and his family could not believe their eyes. After shouts of, "Surprise! Welcome to Leiden!" There stood, right before his eyes, his cousin Chris, Chris' parents, Pieter and his parents, and many other neighbors. It was their tradition to welcome new families to the neighborhood.

Nicholaas was visibly shaken from this amazing experience. Tears welled up in his eyes from the happiness he felt, after seeing Chris. "Hello, I am Pieter, it is very nice to meet you," said Pieter. "Chris has been talking about you non-stop, so I was also anxious to meet you. I understand you are a superb football player. We could use someone like you to play on the 10-12 year olds team," stated Pieter.

"Wow that sounds great! I would love to play football, again!" shouted Nicholaas excitedly. "I could show them a few plays I learned back at home, when I played in Eden Prairie."

"Sure, we can talk more about this later," replied Pieter. "Hey, Nicholaas, Chris gave me an idea about something I think you would like as a welcome home gift."

"Wha...what is it?" stammered Nicholaas, not knowing what to expect.

"Open it!" announced Chris and Pieter, shouting at the same time.

Nicholaas ripped the paper of what appeared to be, a horizontal shaped box. All the guests looked on as Nicholaas opened his present.

"No way!" a shocked and stunned Nicholaas replied. "My very own wooden checker set and carved wooden figures representing the Minnesota Vikings, in purple, and the opposing team in white. Chris mentioned to me, in an email, that you made checker sets, but I had no idea one was meant for me. What a great remembrance of my life in Eden Prairie…and my new life in Leiden. I will treasure this checker set, always. Thank you, thank you, and thank you!" Nicholaas was very appreciative. Each piece was intricately carved out of wood, and then painted to resemble the football team Nicholaas was so passionate about.

"Yes, my Dad is a woodcarver. He has a shop just outside Leiden. He makes wooden shoes and sometimes repairs some of the antique boats. When I am not in school or playing football, I help my Dad, at the shop," said Pieter.

"Chris, do you remember the first time we met at the Exploration Café? You were wearing that T-shirt that had Leiden on it," recalled Nicholaas.

"Yes," said Chris, "since you will be living in Leiden, I want to give you your own Leiden shirt. Here!"

"Wow, that's awesome. Purple is my favorite color because it reminds me of the Minnesota Vikings." Again, tears welled up in Nicholaas' eyes. The kindness that Pieter and Chris demonstrated was more than he could ever have imagined. "Just think if you had not worn that shirt, or if you weren't at the café, I may not have ever met you or Pieter. Look at all the exciting adventures we've had already," Nicholaas continued. "Remember the storm, when the wind was tossing the air balloon like it was a toy?" "And how scared we were." Chris added.

"Yeah, remember when my dad sheltered us so we wouldn't get thrown into the Atlantic Ocean directly below us?"

"The real adventure began when we found that deserted mansion and all the treasures inside of it!" remembered Chris. "Yeah, yeah, and remember the replica of the Metro dome, where the Minnesota Vikings play? When I was on the field, I felt like I was in a real game."

I hope we can go back there someday," suggested Nicholaas. "Hey, Pieter, why don't you come with us, when we plan our trip to Funchal, Madeira Island? We were only in the mansion a short time when we accidentally found a secret passageway…there may be other mysterious rooms, we haven't found, yet!"

"Yes, yes, I would love to visit Funchal, let's plan a trip for the fall, with our parents help, of course!" shouted Pieter, in an enthusiastic and joyful tone.

Nicholaas, have you ever thought about what adventures are waiting right here in Holland? There are many old buildings that were built in the sixteenth and seventeenth centuries, and they're still standing in the Old Town Center…or the Kagerplassen, where you can learn to sail, camp, hike, or visit the windmills on the lake. The Kagerplassen Lake offers a great variety of angelfish, including the Pomcantheus Maculus."

"Wow, there IS a lot to do, in Holland! I can't wait to discover my next adventure with you, Pieter!"

"Reading is the most amazing adventure of all! Reading can take you places that you have never been before". Places you long to visit. Researching and finding out interesting and curious facts makes life fun. As you read this book, you learned some amazing facts about each of the countries you visited through your journey with me. I hope you will continue to travel along by reading the next book in the series. Pieter and I meet up with Chris, in Funchal, Madeira, and travel on to Spain.

Now I will begin compiling notes from my journal to my friends in Eden Prairie, Minnesota. "Although I am far away from them, my heart is with them, always.